HEINEMANN GUIDED READERS
INTERMEDIATE LEVEL

JAMES VANCE MARSHALL

Walkabout

Retold by Jim Alderson

HEINEMANN

Series Editor: John Milne

The Heinemann Guided Readers provide a choice of enjoyable reading material for learners of English. The series is published at five levels – Starter, Beginner, Elementary, Intermediate and Upper. At **Intermediate Level**, the control of content and language has the following main features:

Information Control
Information which is vital to the understanding of the story is presented in an easily assimilated manner and is repeated when necessary. Difficult allusion and metaphor are avoided and cultural backgrounds are made explicit.

Structure Control
Most of the structures used in the Readers will be familiar to students who have completed an elementary course of English. Other grammatical features may occur, but their use is made clear through context and reinforcement. This ensures that the reading, as well as being enjoyable, provides a continual learning situation for the students. Sentences are limited in most cases to a maximum of three clauses and within sentences there is a balanced use of adverbial and adjectival phrases. Great care is taken with pronoun reference.

Vocabulary Control
There is a basic vocabulary of approximately 1,600 words. Help is given to the students in the form of illustrations, which are closely related to the text.

Glossary
Some difficult words and phrases in this book are important for understanding the story. Some of these words are explained in the story, some are shown in the pictures, and others are marked with a number like this . . .[3] Words with a number are explained in the Glossary on page 73.

Contents

A Note About This Story

This story takes place in Australia. It tells how two young children walked fourteen hundred miles from the Sturt Desert to Adelaide. The pictures round this map of Australia show some of the insects and animals that the children saw on their journey.

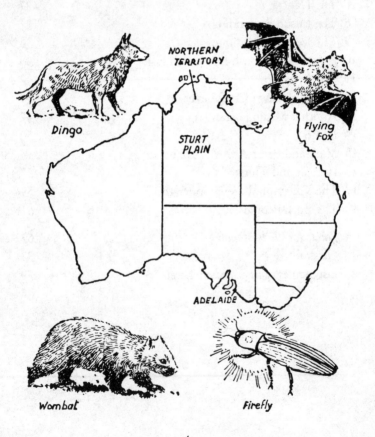

Dingo

NORTHERN TERRITORY

STURT PLAIN

Flying Fox

ADELAIDE

Wombat

Firefly

1

Plane Crash

Mary and Peter were the only passengers in the plane. Mary was thirteen years old and her brother was eight. The children lived in Charleston in the United States of America and they were on their way to visit their Uncle Keith. Uncle Keith lived in the city of Adelaide in Australia.

The two men flying the plane – the pilot and the co-pilot – were in the front, at the controls. The plane was now flying over the Australian desert and the children were feeling happy. They would soon be in Adelaide.

Mary looked out of the window and smiled. It had been a wonderful trip and she had enjoyed every minute of it. She could see the land below and this made her excited. Australia was a completely new country to her. It would be such fun to see what it was like!

Then suddenly the smile went from her face. The plane was making a strange sound. Something was wrong. A few seconds later, she gave a gasp[1] of fear. One of the engines was on fire! She could see flames.

The flames became bigger and bigger. They began to spread[2] along the wing. Mary shouted to the pilot and co-pilot. The two men told her not to worry. They said everything was all right. Then they began to take the plane down as fast as they could. Seconds later, they made a crash landing in the middle of the desert.

When the plane hit the ground, the flames spread everywhere. Mary and Peter got out of the plane as fast as they could. But Peter could not move quickly because his feet kept sinking[3] into the soft, deep sand.

'Quick, Peter!' said Mary. 'Quick, before the plane explodes[4].'

When Mary had got her brother away from the burning plane, she turned round. She saw the co-pilot trying to pull the pilot out of the plane. Suddenly there was an explosion. The heat was terrible. The two men became white hot. Then there was nothing left of them.

Mary turned away. She did not want to see any more. She wanted to forget. It was too horrible.

The two children were now all alone in the middle of the Australian desert.

2

A Night by a Stream

Mary and Peter walked for about half an hour. It was now late afternoon and the sun began to set. Peter was getting tired. His leg hurt him and he was afraid.

Mary was very lucky and found a small stream. When night came, they had a drink of water and sat down near some big rocks.

It was silent and dark. The children were afraid. They lay close together and tried to keep warm. Peter was trembling[5] and moved closer to his sister.

Mary took his hand and held it tightly. 'It's all right, Peter,' she whispered[6]. 'I'm here.'

After a time, the boy stopped trembling. His sister seemed grown-up. He felt safe with her at his side.

'Mary,' he whispered. 'I'm hungry.'

Mary put her hand in the pocket of her dress and pulled out a stick of barley sugar[7]. She broke it into two pieces and gave one piece to Peter. Then she put the other piece back into her pocket. This was the last of their food.

'Don't bite it,' she whispered. 'Suck it.'

They were whispering because it was so silent. The only sound they heard was the stream going over the stones.

The hours passed by very slowly. The night was black and there was no moon. Not a sound could be heard.

At last Peter fell asleep.

But Mary did not sleep. She had to watch out for danger. She had to look after Peter because she was his big sister. Mary loved her brother and had always looked after him. Now they were lost in the middle of Australia. Now she had to be more than a sister to him. She had to be a mother to him as well.

For a time, Mary sat still and kept watch. But the night was dark and warm and her eyelids began to close. Soon she was fast asleep.

As the children slept, the desert around them slowly came to life. In the distance, a dingo – a wild dog – began to bark. Nearby came the flip-flap-flip of the wings of the flying foxes[8]. And fireflies[9] went by shining like tiny lamps.

A wombat[10] came out of its den[11] in the ground and had a good look at the children. Then it went on its way in search of roots and vegetables.

Mary moved about in her sleep. She was dreaming about the plane. She kept seeing the flames and the explosion. And she kept thinking of the two men who had been killed. In her sleep, she held her brother's hand tightly.

Slowly, the sky became less dark. The grey light of dawn was coming from the east. It would soon be the start of a new day.

3

Next Day in the Desert

Next morning, the sun shone down brightly on the Australian desert. Trees, flowers, shrubs[12] and dry grass were growing all around. These were the kinds of plants that had learned to live without much water.

The Australian desert, also known as 'the bush', was full of colour – black, green, white, red and gold. It was a very beautiful sight.

But Mary and Peter did not see the beauty of the bush desert in the early morning. They were still fast asleep.

Then a big grey bird flew onto a tall tree. It was a kookaburra, an ugly bird with a huge beak. The kookaburra was looking for something to eat. The bird saw the sleeping children and screamed loudly.

The noise woke Mary up. She jumped to her feet and her heart was beating fast. Then she saw the kookaburra. It was only a bird, a big ugly bird.

Peter was still asleep. He was lying out of the sunlight, in the shade of a rock. He looked very small and helpless.

Mary began to worry. Peter would be hungry when he woke up. She was hungry too. There was only one piece of barley sugar left now. They could get water from the stream, but what could they eat? If they did not get food, they would die. They would slowly starve to death.

Mary looked at the kookaburra. She wanted to catch the bird and eat it. But the kookaburra seemed to know what the girl was thinking. It gave a loud scream and flew away.

The sun began to get warmer. Mary felt dirty and uncomfortable. She looked at the stream. Little birds were splashing about in the cool, clear water.

Mary saw that Peter was asleep. She looked carefully around. They were all alone. Nobody would see her take off her clothes. Quickly, she kicked the shoes off her feet and pulled her dress over her head. Then she stepped out of her pants and ran naked[13] down to the water.

The water came up over her knees, thighs and waist. The little birds flew quickly away and Mary was all alone in the pool. The water came up to her shoulders before her toes touched the bottom of the pool.

Mary laughed and splashed about in the water. She had forgotten she was hungry.

Peter woke up. He heard the splash of water. Then he saw his sister.

'Hi, Mary!' he yelled[14]. 'I'm coming too.'

He threw off his clothes and jumped into the pool. Water splashed into the air.

Mary was angry. She caught her brother under the arms. She pulled him back to the bank of the stream.

'Peter, you silly fool,' she said. 'It's too deep for you.'

'It's not,' said the boy. 'I know how to swim.'

He jumped into the water again. Mary watched her brother swim. Then she suddenly remembered that she had no clothes on. Very quickly she got out of the pool and put on her dress. She did not like to be seen naked.

Peter watched her. He did not understand. 'You're all wet,' he said. 'You should have dried yourself first.'

'Stop talking, Peter. And dry yourself.'

She helped him out of the pool, and dried him with his shirt.

'I'm hungry,' said Peter. 'What can we eat?'

Mary pulled out the last piece of barley sugar and gave it to him.

'It's not much,' he said. Peter broke off a piece and handed it to his sister.

'It's all right,' she said. 'I've had mine.'

10

Mary watched her brother walk along the stream. He was happy now and his mouth was full of the barley sugar.

Mary was worried. Now they had no food left at all.

4

Looking for Food

Mary watched Peter playing. He was crawling over the sand. Suddenly the little boy jumped to his feet. He held the seat of his trousers and gave a terrible yell of pain.

Mary rushed over to help him. For a while she did not know what had happened. Then she saw what it was. Ants[15]. Jumping ants. The ants were jumping high into the air and biting at Peter's trousers.

Mary pulled off the boy's trousers.

'It's all right,' she said. 'Look – ants! They are hanging onto your trousers. They think you are still inside.'

Peter stopped crying. He looked at his trousers on the ground. It was true. The ants were still there. With a shout of anger he jumped on his trousers. He stamped and stamped. He wanted to kill all the insects.

'It's all right, Peter,' said Mary. 'They are all dead now.' She helped him put on his trousers.

Peter started to cry again. The bites were hurting him. Mary put her arms around him. He felt small and thin. He was trembling. She could hear his heart beating.

'It's all right, Peter,' she whispered. 'I won't let them bite you again.'

He stopped crying, but only for a moment. Then he started crying again.

'What's wrong, Peter?'

'I don't like this place.'

Mary took a deep breath. This was what she had been afraid of. She knew what Peter was going to say next. But there was nothing she could do.

'I don't like it here,' said Peter. 'I want to go home.'

'But we can't go home, Peter,' she said. 'We've got nothing to cross the sea in.'

'Then let's go to Uncle Keith. In Adelaide.'

Mary was surprised that Peter had remembered all this. 'All right,' she said slowly. 'I'll take you to Uncle Keith.'

He stopped crying immediately. 'When? Now?' he asked.

'Yes,' she said. 'We'll go now. We'll start to walk to Adelaide.'

The children did not know that Adelaide was fourteen hundred miles away. They were in the middle of a desert. If they stayed by the plane someone might find them. But they did not know this. They started to walk.

They walked along beside the stream for two hours. Then the little boy began to slow down. When Mary saw this she stopped.

'We'll rest now,' she said.

Peter sat down. He was very tired. Mary pushed the hair out of his eyes and wiped his hot face.

For a long time, there was silence. Then came the question the girl had been afraid of.

'I'm hungry, Mary. What are we going to eat?'

'Oh, Peter! It's not dinner time yet.'

'When *will* it be dinner time?'

'I'll tell you when,' said Mary.

But Peter was getting worried.

'When it *is* dinner time,' he said, 'what are we going to eat?'

'I'll find something,' she said.

But Mary was very worried. She had been looking for berries[16] to eat, but she had not found any.

'I'm hungry now,' Peter said.

Quickly she got up.

'All right,' she said. 'Let's look for something to eat.'

———

At first they were happy – looking for food was like a game. They looked for fish in the stream. But the fish were asleep under the mud[17]. The birds had flown away and the animals were asleep in their holes. The children found nothing to eat at all. It was midday and it was very hot. The animals in the desert did not stay out in the sun at midday.

Then Peter had an idea. He pointed to some nearby hills.

'Mary!'

'Yes, Peter?'

'Let's climb to the top of that mountain. We might be able to see the sea from there.'

It took them a long time to climb the hill. The sun had almost set when they got to the top. They saw miles and miles of desert. Nothing but desert. But in the distance, Peter saw some silver pools. These silver pools shone very brightly in the sun.

Peter jumped with joy.

'Look, Mary look!' he shouted. 'It's the sea! We haven't far to go.'

Mary caught hold of him. She held him tight and pressed his face against her breast.

'Don't look, Peter,' she said. 'Don't look again.'

Mary sat down. She did not want Peter to see how upset she was. She knew what the pools of silver were. It was salt. She knew they were in the middle of the Australian desert. She began to squeeze her hands together. She knew they were lost.

After a long time she got up. She took Peter back down to the stream. There was water there.

Peter was angry. 'Let's go to the sea!' he said.

'We'll go tomorrow,' said Mary.

'When will we eat?'

'Tomorrow,' said Mary. 'Tomorrow we'll eat. We won't be hungry any more.'

But she was afraid. She was going mad with hunger. If they did not get food soon, they would die.

———

Next morning, the children woke up early. Peter wanted to go to the sea. But Mary said they must find some food first. They looked for food all morning. They went far away from the stream, searching for fruit. They looked at all kinds of trees and bushes. But the hours went by and they found nothing to eat. Then suddenly they saw a group of beautiful trees with thick, silver-coloured leaves. Peter gave a shout of joy. He could see red and green fruit hanging from the branches.

'Peter!' yelled Mary. 'Don't eat them! They might be poisonous[18]!'

But Peter did not listen to her. He ran up to the trees and began to push the fruit into his mouth. Seconds later, Mary was doing the same.

The fruits were sweet. The two starving children ate and ate and ate.

For a long time after, Mary and Peter sat in the shade of the trees. These trees had saved their lives. The children were too happy to speak.

After a while, Mary began to pick some more of the fruit. They would need this food on their journey to Adelaide. She put the fruit in Peter's handkerchief and put some more in the pockets of her dress. Peter also got up. He began to pick some fruit as well. Suddenly he began to feel nervous[19]. The bushes and trees were silent, but Peter was afraid. He crept back to his sister.

'Mary!' he whispered. 'I think someone is watching us.'

'What?' said Mary. 'Someone watching us? Where?'

The girl turned round. There was a boy standing two metres away from her. He was so near she could almost reach out and touch him. She dropped the fruit into the grass and almost screamed with fright[20]. The boy had dark skin and he had no clothes on at all!

5

The Bush Boy

At first Mary wanted to grab[21] Peter and run away. But slowly she became less and less afraid. The boy was about the same age as herself and he had no weapons[22]. He did not look dangerous. He was standing there looking at them curiously.

The bush boy did not look like an African-American. His skin was black, but his hair was straight. And his eyes were blue-black.

There was a boy standing two metres away from her.

In his hands, he held the dead body of a baby wallaby[23].

Mary was not afraid. She was not worried by the dead animal. But she could not understand why the bush boy was naked. It seemed shocking[24] and wrong to her.

The three children stood looking at each other in the middle of the Australian desert. They did not move. They stared[25] at each other in surprise. They were like people from different worlds.

And they were from different worlds.

Mary and Peter were from America. They came from a land of machines and education. People had always taken care of them. They had not yet learned to look after themselves. They did not know anything about life in the desert and they were helpless.

But the bush boy was different. His people – the Australian Aborigines – had lived in the desert for twenty thousand years. Their lives were simple. They had no machines to help them, no homes, no crops[26], no clothes, no possessions. The Aborigines walked from one water-hole to the next. When they had eaten all the food in one place, they moved on to another. They knew that death was their enemy. They knew how to keep themselves alive in the middle of the desert.

The hot sun shone down on the children. They kept on staring at each other. They stared and stared and stared.

Mary had decided not to move. She would keep staring at this black boy. She would stare at him until he understood that his nakedness was wrong. Then he would go away. She pushed out her chin and stared as hard as she could.

Peter decided to do the same as his sister. He held her hand and waited for something to happen.

But the bush boy was in no hurry. He had caught his food and there was water nearby. He was going to have a good look at these strange creatures[27]. They were the first white people he had ever seen. He knew they were not dangerous because they had no weapons.

Mary stared even harder at the bush boy, but Peter began to

move restlessly. He moved his head and began to cough.

Then he sneezed.

It was a very loud sneeze. He gave a second sneeze even louder than the first. Peter could not stop.

Suddenly the bush boy began to laugh. At first it was a quiet laugh. Then it became louder and louder. Mary watched in amazement[28]. The bush boy could not stop laughing. He lay on the ground and laughed and laughed.

Soon Peter began to laugh too. Seconds later, he was lying on the ground as well.

Mary watched them. A year ago, she would have joined in the fun. But not now. She felt she was not a child any more. She was too grown-up. She frowned[29] and took Peter by the hand.

'Stop it, Peter,' she said. 'That's enough.'

The two boys stopped laughing. There was silence for a moment, then the bush boy spoke.

'Worumgala?' (Where do you come from?)

Mary and Peter looked at each other. They did not understand.

The bush boy tried again.

'Worum mwa?' (Where are you going?)

It was Peter who tried to speak to the bush boy.

'We don't know what you're talking about, but we're lost. We want to go to Adelaide. That's where Uncle Keith lives. Which way do we go?'

The bush boy grinned[30]. He thought Peter's voice was strange and funny. The bush boy grinned again and Peter grinned back. He wanted to start laughing again.

But the bush boy did not want to laugh now. He went up to Peter and touched the boy's face with his fingers. Then he looked at his fingers. He was surprised because there was no white colour on them. Next, he touched Peter's red hair. Again he was surprised. There was no red colour on his fingers. Then he looked at the white boy's clothes.

He touched Peter's red hair. He was surprised. There was no red colour on his fingers.

Peter suddenly felt very important. He knew that the bush boy had never seen anything like him before. He stood up straight and let the bush boy touch his clothes.

The bush boy pulled at Peter's shirt and then he looked at Peter's trousers.

'Those are trousers,' said Peter. 'Short trousers. You should have trousers too. Haven't you any shops here?'

But the bush boy was not listening. He had found the elastic that held the boy's trousers up. While he touched it, the white boy kept on talking.

'That's elastic, that is. It holds your trousers up. It stretches. Look!'

Peter pulled the elastic forward and then let it fly back. The loud noise made the bush boy jump. Peter was pleased with himself and did it again. The bush boy grinned and then had a look at Peter's shoes.

Then he turned to Mary.

The girl knew that soon the bush boy would look at her. She felt very frightened.

Mary stood completely still. She did not move away from the bush boy. Her heart was beating fast. She was terribly afraid of being touched by a naked black boy. But she did not move. The black fingers touched her body.

But he soon stopped. The big creature was like the smaller one. He stepped back. There was nothing more he wanted to know.

The bush boy turned round and picked up the dead wallaby. Some ants were running in the wallaby's fur. The boy knocked the ants off the wallaby and walked away. Soon he was out of sight.

Mary and Peter were shocked. They could not believe that the bush boy had gone. Peter was the first to understand what had happened.

'Mary!' he said in a frightened voice. 'He's gone!'

The girl said nothing. She was pleased that the naked black

boy had gone away. But she was sorry that she had not asked him for help. She held her face in her hands. What were they going to do now? Who was going to help them?

It was Peter who decided what was to be done. He liked the laughing bush boy, and he was not going to lose him.

'Mary!' he gasped. 'Come on. After him!'

He ran into the bush. His sister followed him slowly. She was still afraid of the bush boy.

'Hey!' yelled Peter. 'We want to come too. Wait for us!'

'Hey!' yelled Peter again, as he ran after him. 'Wait for us. Wait for us. Wait for us.'

6

The Journey

The bush boy turned. He had heard the shout. He stood and waited for the strangers to come.

The bush boy was not afraid of the strangers. The boy was not afraid, but he was surprised. What did the strangers want?

Peter ran up to the bush boy.

'Don't leave us!' he said. 'We're lost. We want food and drink. And we want to know how to get to Adelaide.'

The bush boy smiled. He thought Peter's voice was funny. This made Mary angry. She took hold of Peter's hand and tried to pull him away. But Peter would not move away with her. He knew they needed help. He was going to ask for help.

'Look,' he said, 'we're lost. We want water. You know what water is, don't you? Wa-ter. Wa-ter.'

He held his hands together and put them to his lips. Then he pretended[31] to drink.

The bush boy nodded. 'Arkooloola,' he said.

The bush boy was serious now. He knew all about thirst.

'Arkooloola.' He said the word again. The word was soft and musical. He licked his lips and he pretended to drink as well.

Peter was delighted. 'That's it,' he said. 'You've got[32] it. Arkooloola. That's what we want. And food too. You understand? Food. Foo-ood. Foo-ood.'

Peter pretended to cut things up with a knife and fork. Then he pretended to chew[33].

The bush boy did not understand the movement for knife and fork. But he understood the chewing. 'Yeemara,' he said.

The white boy danced with joy. 'You've got it!' he said. 'Yeemara and arkooloola. That's what we want. Now where do we find them?'

The bush boy turned and moved away from the children. Then he stopped and looked back.

'Kurura,' he said.

Peter became excited. 'Come on, Mary,' he said. 'Kurura means "follow me".'

Slowly, unhappily, the girl followed.

———

After a short time, they came to a thick forest[34]. It was dark and cool in this forest.

Peter had to run because the bush boy walked so quickly. Sweat ran round Peter's eyes and fell into his mouth. His hair and clothes were wet with sweat. He walked more and more slowly.

Mary stopped and waited for Peter. The small boy held her hand. The girl was happy now. Peter was her brother and she would look after him. She did not want Peter to go running after a bush boy.

'All right, Peter,' she whispered, 'we won't leave you behind.'

The two white children were very hungry and thirsty. They had been walking for many hours.

Suddenly the forest came to an end. There was no more shade in front of them. All they could see was desert. Mile after mile of hot, burning sand, mile after mile of salt and hard rocks. This was the Sturt Desert, a place without food or water.

'Kurura,' said the bush boy. Then he began to walk into the desert.

Mary did not follow the bush boy. She stopped. How far away would the food and water be? Perhaps it would be too far away for her and Peter. She sat down in the shade and Peter sat down beside her. The little boy was exhausted[35]. Sweat fell from his hair.

The bush boy came back. He spoke quietly to the children. He looked very worried. They would die if they did not keep walking. The evil spirits[36] would come to take their bodies. He pointed to some rocks in the distance. There was food and water near those rocks. The children must follow him.

Mary knew what the bush boy was trying to say. But she did not want to follow him. She wanted to stay in the shade. The rocks were too far away. How could there be water in that place?

'Arkooloola,' said the bush boy. He said the word again and again and kept pointing at the rocks.

Mary looked again at the rocks. Suddenly she smiled. She could see trees and bushes. Perhaps there *was* water there. She stood up. 'Come on, Peter,' she said.

Peter was very tired and Mary had to help him. It was late afternoon when they reached the rocks. They came to some ferns[37] and soon they heard the sound of water.

Peter did not want Mary to help him any more. He began to run forward by himself. He ran into the tall ferns. Moments later, Mary heard him shout out with excitement.

'It's water, Mary! Water.'

'Arkooloola,' said the bush boy and grinned.

The white girl and the black boy pushed their way through the tall ferns. Soon they came to a small pool of water.

Peter was flat on his stomach. His head was in the pool and the water came right up to his ears. In a second, Mary was down beside him. Both children drank, and drank.

The water was warm and did not taste very nice. As the girl drank, she watched the bush boy. The bush boy was not drinking from the top of the pool. He put his hand to the bottom of the pool and took up handfuls of water. Mary did the same. The water from the bottom was cool and delicious.

The bush boy drank only a little. Soon he got to his feet and climbed onto a rock. He sat in the warm light of the setting sun and watched the strangers. He was curious about them. They were so helpless. Unless he looked after them, they would die.

Peter had finished drinking. He stood up and began to climb towards the bush boy. The bush boy leant down and pulled Peter onto the rock.

The drink had made Peter feel much better. He was feeling

hungry now. He had come to ask for food. Peter looked at the baby wallaby in the bush boy's hand. He reached out and gently touched the dead animal.

'Eat?' he asked. 'Yeemara?'

———

The two boys climbed down from the rock. The sun was setting. In half an hour it would be quite dark.

The bush boy moved quickly. He found a good place to make a fire. He began to clear the ground. He brushed away all the leaves, twigs[38] and grass with his hands. He did not want the evil spirits of the bush fire to feed upon them.

Peter watched the bush boy. He was curious. Then he started to do the same. He began to brush away leaves and grass. All the time, he kept asking questions.

'What are you trying to do? Why are you clearing away the twigs and stuff?'

The bush boy grinned. He put a dry leaf and a piece of dry stick on the palm of his hand. Then he began to blow on them.

'Larana,' he said.

'I get it!' Peter shouted. 'Fire. You're going to light a fire.'

'Larana,' the bush boy repeated.

'OK,' said Peter. 'Larana. You're going to light a larana. I'll help you.'

Peter ran about and picked up bits of leaves and grass. The bush boy was very pleased with Peter and grinned.

Mary sat by the side of the pool and watched them. They had forgotten all about her. She felt jealous[39]. She wished she was a boy too! She lay down on the rocks and watched them.

The bush boy took a large, flat piece of wood and cut a hole in it. Then he put some dry twigs and leaves in the hole. Next he took a long, thin stick and put one end into the hole in the wood. Finally, he put the palms of his hands on either side of the long, thin stick. He rubbed his hands backwards and forwards.

Soon the wood became hot. Smoke could be seen. The bush boy rubbed faster and faster. The wood became hotter and hotter, then burst into flames. The boys put on more sticks. The fire was made.

The bush boy cooked the wallaby slowly. An hour later they were eating it in the moonlight. The meat was delicious.

After the meal, the bush boy put out the fire. Then he stood and listened for danger. At last the bush boy was satisfied. He lay down on a rock near the others.

Clouds came along and covered up the moon. The children slept.

7

The Dance

The girl woke early. She lay on her back and watched the light get brighter and brighter. Soon the moon and stars disappeared. It was morning.

Mary stared upwards at the sky. Was there another life far away above the sky? She would know the answer to that question when she was dead. But for the moment she was alive – thanks to the bush boy.

Mary turned and looked at the naked bush boy. She wished she was a boy too!

Mary was still very worried. The bush boy had saved[40] their lives. He knew how to live in the desert. If they stayed with him they would find food and water. But they would still be lost. Could she get the bush boy to take them to Adelaide? But perhaps he did not know where Adelaide was.

More and more questions came into her head. Why was the bush boy all alone in the desert? Where were his people? She could not think of an answer to these questions. She fell asleep again.

A few hours later, she woke up. She heard the sound of laughter and splashing water. Her brother and the bush boy were playing in the pool.

'Come on Mary!' shouted Peter. 'Come in with us.'

'Later,' she shouted, 'when it's warmer.'

The bush boy climbed out of the water. Then he stopped. He had seen something in the sand. He pushed the sand away with his feet and took out a soft, brown ball.

'Worwora!' he said. His voice was excited.

Peter came out of the water. He looked at the ball and touched it.

'Yeemara?' he asked.

The bush boy nodded and they walked away to dig out more of these balls.

Mary waited until the boys were out of sight. Then she took off her clothes and jumped in the pool. Soon she was laughing and splashing in the water. But she listened carefully. When she heard the boys' voices she ran out of the water. She quickly pulled on her dress.

The boys' arms were filled with the soft, brown balls. Mary was suddenly shocked: the bush boy and Peter were both naked! She picked up her brother's trousers from the side of the pool.

'Peter,' she said, 'come here.'

He came slowly towards Mary.

'I don't need clothes, Mary. It's too hot.'

'Put them on,' she said.

Mary sounded just like a teacher.

Peter had always done what his sister told him. But he felt different here in the desert. He stared at Mary for a long time.

'All right,' he said at last. 'I'll wear the trousers, but nothing else.'

A week ago Mary would have been very angry with Peter. But things were different now. The boy put on his trousers and threw the rest of his clothes away.

They cooked the brown balls and they tasted good.

During the meal, Mary watched the bush boy. He had saved their lives. He was healthy and clean. But he was naked and this still shocked her. She wished he would wear a pair of trousers!

Mary suddenly had an idea. She would do something to help the bush boy. She went to the other side of a rock. She pulled up her dress and took off her pants.

Then she walked across to the bush boy and gave him her pants. Mary felt kind and good.

The bush boy took them, but he did not know what they were for. He looked at the present[41]. Then he began to pull the elastic.

'Put them on,' said Peter. 'Put one foot in here. And one foot in there. Then pull them up.'

The bush boy did not understand what Peter was saying. But he understood Peter's movements. He put the pants on.

Mary was happy. The bush boy was no longer naked.

But Peter began to laugh. The bush boy was wearing girl's pants. Peter jumped up and down and pointed at the pants.

'Look! Look! He's wearing a girl's pants.'

Peter laughed and danced up and down. 'Girl's pants! Girl's pants!' he shouted.

Mary was shocked. But the bush boy was pleased. Now he knew why he had been given the present. They wanted him to dance!

Suddenly the bush boy ran and jumped all round the pool. He picked up a stick and used it as a spear[42]. Then he began to dance.

The dance was slow at first, but then it became faster and faster. Sweat ran down the body of the bush boy. On and on he danced. His heart was beating fast. Then suddenly he came to the last part of the dance. He fell onto the ground and turned over and over. At last he stopped. He stood up and looked at the children.

There was silence. The bush boy was naked again. The elastic had broken in the last part of the dance. The pants lay under his feet, stamped into the desert sand.

Mary and the bush boy stared at each other. White girl and black boy.

The girl stared, her eyes opened wider and wider.

The bush boy's eyes opened wider too. He was shocked. He saw for the first time that the larger of the strangers was not a boy. She was a lubra, a young girl. Soon she would be a gin, a fully grown woman.

Sweat ran down the body of the bush boy.
On and on he danced.

The bush boy took a step forward. Then he stopped. The girl's eyes were filled with terror[43]. The bush boy had only seen terror like this twice before. This terror meant only one thing. The girl had seen the Spirit of Death[44] in his eyes! His body began to shake. He was going to die. He knew he was going to die.

8

The Misunderstanding

The bush boy's people were only afraid of one thing. And that was death.

Death was a terrible thing to the bush boy. His people believed that death was the end. They did not believe in a life after death. Death was the end of everything.

That is why the bush boy was so afraid. He was trembling and his body was as cold as ice. Sweat covered his whole body. The girl had looked into his eyes and she had seen the Spirit of Death!

Peter did not understand. First he looked at the bush boy and then at his sister. What had happened? What was wrong? Peter was a helpless little boy again. Suddenly he started to cry.

Now the bush boy was completely certain he was going to die. The little one had seen the Spirit of Death too. So the bush boy turned away. He left the food at the side of the pool. He left the pants in the sand near the fire.

He slowly walked away into the desert.

Mary and Peter watched him go. They did not know that the bush boy had been on his Walkabout.

A Walkabout is a test for Aborigine boys of thirteen or fourteen. They must walk all alone from one water hole to another. They must search for food alone. The journey lasts six to eight months. Only the strongest boys will live. Only the strongest boys will become fathers of children.

Before he met the children, the bush boy had done very well. But now his Walkabout was finished. The Spirit of Death was in his eyes. He was going to die. He would not live to become a man, and he would never have a wife.

––––

Mary and Peter watched the bush boy as he walked slowly into the desert. The girl's face was very pale and she was breathing quickly. The little boy was shocked and frightened. He did not understand what had happened. But Peter understood one thing: the bush boy was leaving them for the second time.

Suddenly the little boy ran into the desert.

'Hey!' His voice was frightened. 'Come back! Come back!'

The bush boy kept on walking. He did not seem to hear.

But Peter was not going to let the bush boy go away. He pulled at the bush boy's legs and grabbed him by the knees.

'Don't leave us,' he said.

The bush boy had to stop. He put his hands gently on Peter's shoulders and tried to push him away. But Peter would not let go.

'Don't leave us,' he said again and again. 'Don't leave us. Don't leave us.'

The bush boy looked at Peter. He let Peter look into his eyes. He wanted the little boy to see the Spirit of Death. Then the little boy would run away in terror.

The two boys stared into each other's eyes. But the bush boy was amazed. The little one did not move away or give a cry of terror.

The bush boy did not understand. Suddenly he felt hope. Perhaps the girl was wrong. Perhaps the Spirit of Death had left him and gone somewhere else.

He turned round and went back to the pool.

But the girl moved away from him. Once again, her eyes were filled with terror.

The bush boy lost all hope. He was going to die. He might not die today, or tomorrow, or the next day. But he would die soon. He would die before the coming of the rains. He would not see his people again.

The bush boy began to think about the two strangers. When he died, they would die too. They were helpless creatures. The Spirit of Death would come for three people and not just one. What was he to do?

The bush boy closed his eyes for a few moments, then he opened them again. He knew now what he had to do. He must lead the strangers to safety. He must take them to the end of his Walkabout. This was the Valley-of-waters-under-the-earth. And they must get there quickly.

'Kurura,' he said, and started to walk across the desert.

The little one followed him immediately. But the girl did not

33

move. The bush boy thought she was going to stay beside the pool. Then he saw her walking after him. But she was a long way behind.

9

The Journey Continues

The Australian desert is not completely flat. There is sand and rocks, water-holes, and many trees and plants.

The bush boy knew where he was going. His people had been here eight years ago when he had been a very little boy. He remembered everything.

Soon they came to a valley. There were many different trees here. In the trees there were thousands of birds.

The children went further into the valley, and they heard a strange noise. It was the noise of a pardalote. They heard the bird's strange cry. The cry sounded like the words, 'It isn't yours. It isn't yours.'

The children looked up. At first they could see nothing. Then a bird flew over their heads and landed on the branch of a tree near them.

'It isn't yours. It isn't yours,' cried the pardalote.

The bush boy knew they would soon come to water. The pardalote always lives by a pool. Soon the children arrived at a small pool near some ferns.

It was midday. The sun was hot and the boys took handfuls of water and splashed them over their heads. Mary did the same. But she would not go near the bush boy. And whenever he looked at her, she moved away in fear.

Peter asked why she was frightened. But she did not reply. Peter went and lay down beside the bush boy in the shade of a rock.

They stayed by the pool for three hours until it became cooler. Then the bush boy got up. Soon they were walking through the valley again.

They walked fifteen miles that day. The bush boy could have walked twice as far, but Peter became tired very quickly. Also the little boy's feet hurt because he had thrown away his shoes.

Late in the evening, they came out of the valley. There were not so many trees and birds now. But three birds, called bustards, followed the children. The bustards were stupid creatures. The bush boy moved back towards the foolish birds. Suddenly his hand went out and he grabbed a baby bustard and killed it.

The bush boy took the bustard to the girl. Then he put the bird into her arms. Among his people the women always carried things.

Mary was shocked. The body of the bird was still moving. Blood fell on the girl's dress. But she did not drop the bird.

35

She held it tightly. But she wanted to be sick every time the bird moved.

Peter saw that his sister was unhappy.

'Give me the bird, Mary,' he said. 'I'll carry it for you.'

He tried to take the bird from her, but the girl turned away.

'It's heavy,' she whispered. 'I'll carry it.'

That night they camped beside some rocks. The two boys found some wood and made a fire. Soon the bustard was cooking.

The bush boy used sign language[45]. Peter nodded. He was beginning to understand the bush boy very well. They were going to eat the bustard in the morning.

Later, they lay down to go to sleep. The girl was still nervous. She kept moving about. She wanted to keep far away from the bush boy. Peter was very tired and wanted to sleep.

'Stop moving about, Mary,' he said. 'I can't get to sleep.'

'Sorry, Peter.'

For a while there was silence. The bush boy moved quietly about the camp. Mary watched him and started to move around again. 'Peter!' she said. Her voice was quiet and frightened.

'Yes?'

'Come and lie beside me. Please.'

'Why?'

'I'm cold.' Peter moved slowly across and the two children lay close beside one another together.

The girl lay by the fire where she could see the bush boy. The bush boy was standing on one foot and staring into the moonlit valley. Mary watched him carefully. What was he thinking about? Was he waiting for her to fall asleep?

'I won't sleep,' she said to herself. 'Not till he does.' She said it over and over again. 'Not till he does. Not till he does.'

But at last her eyes started to close and she fell asleep. But the bush boy did not sleep. Hour after hour, he stood there in silence. The bush boy was thinking about death.

The Australian Aborigine people are very strong. They can live in the desert where it is very hot during the day and very cold at night. But the bush people have a terrible weakness. When the bush people believe they are going to die, nothing can save them. Many strong, healthy bush people have died because someone has told them that they were going to die. White doctors have tried to keep them alive, but the bush people have always slowly died.

The bush boy knew that he was going to die. He had seen the terror in the girl's eyes. He had seen the same terror twice before. Long ago, he had seen a woman who had given birth to a dead child. He had seen the terror in her eyes. And once an old man had been too weak to walk. So his people had left him to die alone in a waterless desert. And the bush boy still remembered the terror in the old man's eyes.

So the bush boy stood in silence. He was waiting. He stared across the moonlit valley. He wondered how and when the Spirit of Death would come to take him away.

10

Peter and the Bush Boy Catch Fish

In the morning, they ate the bustard which had cooked in the fire. Peter and Mary ate the meat slowly, but the bush boy wanted to move. He put out the fire and began to walk away. He walked quickly.

Mary was worried about Peter. She thought he might not be able to go as quickly as the bush boy. But Peter had slept well and felt strong. He walked beside the bush boy and kept asking questions. The bush boy seemed to understand Peter and was answering all his questions.

Peter was learning how to speak the bush boy's language. He held up a piece of rock to the bush boy.

'What do you call this?'

'Garsha.' The word sounded hard like rock.

'And this?' The white boy picked up some grass.

'Karathara.' The word sounded soft like the wind blowing through long grass.

'Garsha. Karathara. Garsha. Karathara.' The little boy said the words again and again. He went looking for more things to show the bush boy. He kept asking questions, hour after hour. Mary felt lonely.

They began to walk across a plateau[46] of red dust. It was not easy walking on the plateau. It was very hot and there was no water. Peter began to walk more slowly. The dust made Peter sneeze.

The bush boy became worried. Had the little one caught the fever-that-comes-with-the-rains?

In fact, Peter had a cold. And the red dust of the plateau was making his cold worse and worse.

They walked across the plateau and the little boy sneezed, and sneezed, and sneezed. When they stopped for the night, he was exhausted. He was too tired to eat. He went up to his sister and lay down beside her. Then he went to sleep.

The bush boy quickly made a fire. He was pleased. They had walked seventeen miles that day. After seven more days they would arrive at the Valley-of-waters-under-the-earth. When they got there, the strangers would be safe.

He did not go near the girl. He did not know why the girl wanted him to stay away from her. Perhaps she thought the Spirit of Death might go from him to her. So the bush boy lay down quietly on the other side of the fire.

As he was going to sleep, he gave a sudden sneeze.

———

The next day, the bush boy was the first to wake up. He got up and walked quietly down the valley.

Peter woke next. He sat up. Then he rubbed his hands over his eyes and nose. He had no handkerchief, so he sniffed[47]. It was a very loud sniff.

Mary sat up and looked at him. She was angry.

'Where's your handkerchief, Peter?'

'I've lost it.'

Peter got up quickly and said, 'I'm going to look for the boy. Are you coming?'

Mary shook her head and lay down again. She looked unhappy and Peter did not know why.

The little boy walked off. He put his hands in the pockets of his trousers and sniffed loudly. Suddenly, the little boy stopped. He could hear a strange noise. Very carefully and quietly, he walked up to some rocks and looked over.

There was a small pool six metres below him. It had rocks all around it. The bush boy was at the side of the pool. He was pushing a large stone about the size of a football. When he saw Peter he grinned.

'Yarrawa!' he said, and pointed to the pool.

Peter came down the rocks. He saw the yarrawa at once. They were small fish. The little boy suddenly remembered he was hungry. He had not yet had his breakfast.

'Yeemara?' he said, pointing to the fish.

The bush boy nodded.

Peter walked into the water. He could see the fish quite clearly; there were hundreds of them. He put his hands in the water and tried to catch them. But the fish swam quickly and easily away. The bush boy laughed. And Peter came out of the pool. The bush boy gave Peter a small stone.

'Kurura,' said the bush boy. He began to push his large stone up some rocks above the pool. Then he pushed his stone into the pool, and Peter did the same. There was a loud splash. The rocks hit the water; it was like an explosion. The fish came floating up to the surface of the water.

The bush boy jumped into the pool and Peter followed him. Together, they grabbed the fish and threw them onto the rocks.

The bush boy was delighted. He climbed out of the pool and began to pick up the fish. But the fish were difficult to hold. Peter took off his trousers. The boys wrapped the fish in the trousers and carried them back to the fire.

When the children had finished eating, Peter would not put his trousers on again. Mary was very angry.

'Feel the trousers,' the little boy said. 'They're wet and horrible.'

'Wash them and put them on,' his sister told him.

'No!'

Peter was not going to do what she said.

The bush boy was ready to move again. They needed the yarrawa for food; he was not going to leave the fish behind. He wrapped them in the little boy's trousers and gave the trousers to the girl.

'Kurura,' he said.

And so they began the fourth day of the Walkabout.

11

The Lyre Bird

The children came to some flat ground and the bush boy
moved more quickly. After a few hours, Peter's cold became
worse and his nose began to run. He was very pleased to rest in the
shade of some trees.

But soon the children were on their way again. They walked
on and on. On and on.

Half way through the afternoon, something remarkable[48]
happened.

The bush boy suddenly stopped. He stood still for over half
a minute. Then he walked carefully and quietly forward towards
some bushes. Mary and Peter followed him and stared through the
leaves.

They saw a bird. They saw an ordinary, brown bird. The bird
looked sad and had a straggling tail. The bird was looking for
insects. The white children were disappointed. But the black boy
made them wait quietly.

Suddenly the bird stared to sing and he was no longer
ordinary. For his song was the most beautiful thing they had
ever heard. On and on went the song and the children listened
silently.

The song stopped. And then the ordinary, brown bird
suddenly changed into a beautiful creature. The straggling tail
opened up and it was blue, silver and gold. Then the bird started
to sing again. This time, he danced joyfully from side to side.

Then it all ended. The dance and the singing stopped. He was
just another ordinary bird again, looking for insects.

The children walked on. The sun moved lower. The sky was
red and gold.

As the sun set, the children stopped under some trees. The

bush boy made a fire and the children sat down beside it. Peter moved away from the smoke of the fire and sneezed again. But he was not sneezing so much now. His cold was getting better.

The bush boy had gone into the darkness. Suddenly he came back into the firelight. He was holding three small branches. He was pretending to be the brown bird. The branches were the wings and the tail. Then he began to sing and dance like the lyre bird. He danced round and round the fire.

Mary and Peter were delighted and they laughed and laughed. They stamped their feet and clapped their hands.

43

Then suddenly, in the middle of his dance, the bush boy sneezed. He sneezed again and again.

The bush boy suddenly grew weak. He put his hand to his forehead and his fingers were wet. He was afraid. He remembered how an old man had once sneezed. The old man's forehead had become wet and he had died soon after.

The bush boy lay close to the fire, but he could not stop sneezing and shivering[49].

The white children looked at the bush boy in amazement. But neither of them went over to him. The girl did not want to go near him. And Peter was very tired. Soon Peter and his sister were fast asleep.

But the bush boy did not sleep for many hours. He lay close to the fire, but he could not stop shivering. And he sneezed again and again.

12

The Bush Boy Gets Weaker

Next morning, the bush boy had caught Peter's cold. His nose was running and his body felt painful. The sun came up and the white children waited for him to move.

But the bush boy stayed sitting on the ground, hour after hour.

'Mary!' The little boy was worried. 'I think he's ill.'

'He looks all right to me.'

'I think I'll ask him.' Peter went up to the bush boy.

'Hey! Are you all right? If you're all right, let's start walking to Adelaide.'

The bush boy looked up. He saw the two children staring at him. He remembered the Valley-of-waters-under-the-earth was still five days' walk away. Slowly, he got to his feet. Without saying a word, he set off towards the south.

All that morning they walked in silence.

A little after midday, the bush boy went off on a search for food. He found fourteen eggs in a nest. The children cooked the eggs and ate them. The eggs made them thirsty, but there was no water.

The midday rest was longer than usual. The white children had to ask the bush boy to start walking. His cold was worse now. His nose was running; his eyes were almost closed; he was sneezing and coughing. When he started off at last, he walked slowly.

'Mary!' The little boy was worried. 'He's not well[50]. You've got to do something.'

'He's got a cold, Peter,' Mary replied. 'He caught it from you. It's nothing to worry about.'

'But look at his eyes. They look strange. Something's wrong.'

But the girl would not look at the bush boy's eyes.

'He's all right,' she said. 'Don't worry.'

They walked all afternoon and all evening. They found a water-hole, but it was dried up. They found another water-hole. The water was dirty and tasted of salt. But the children drank it.

The bush boy was too tired to make a fire. The children found some wood by themselves. Then they asked the bush boy to light it. After this, the three children lay down to sleep. They were all exhausted. Peter and Mary went to sleep quickly, but the bush boy stayed awake hour after hour. One minute he felt hot, and the next minute he felt cold. He had a fever.

At midnight, the bush boy felt his forehead and his fingers were wet. He started to tremble. He was afraid. Did the two strangers know how to build a burial platform[51]? It must be high off the ground or the evil spirits would come and take his body.

Next day, the children moved on again. They had no breakfast and the bush boy was getting weaker all the time. They began to walk across a flat plain[52]. They saw some hills in the distance. The bush boy pointed to the hills.

'Arkooloola,' he said.

They walked on and on. For a long time, the children did not seem to be getting nearer to the hills. But at last the children arrived in the shade of the hills.

They stopped beside some long pools of water and sat down. The bush boy was not coughing and sneezing so much now. But he was getting weaker and weaker.

Peter tried to help him. He saw that the bush boy was trembling. Peter picked up his trousers and tried to cover the bush boy. Suddenly Peter had an idea.

'Mary!' Peter shouted. 'He's cold. Why don't you give him your dress?'

Mary was shocked. For a moment she stared at her brother. Then she turned away and started to throw wood on the fire.

But the little boy asked again. 'Come on, Mary! Don't be selfish[53]. He's cold.'

The girl said nothing.

Peter looked at her curiously. Her face had gone white. Her eyes were frightened.

'I think you're afraid!' he said. 'Cowardly[54] girl! Cowardly girl!'

Mary turned away. She held her face in her hands. She wished he was a few years older. Then he would understand.

She saw the bush boy looking at her, and then she shivered.

Mary threw some sticks onto the fire. The stars shone in the sky. The three children lay down and slept.

13

Another Misunderstanding

Next morning, Peter woke up early. He went over to the billabongs[55]. The water looked cool. The little boy found a deep pool and jumped in. At one end of the pool, there was a waterfall[56].

After a time, Peter came back to the fire.

The bush boy was still asleep, but Mary had woken up. Peter told her about the billabong and the clear, cool water.

The girl looked at the bush boy and saw he was asleep.

'You look after the fire, Peter,' she said. 'Can you do that while I wash myself?'

'All right.'

Mary smiled at Peter and went over to the far side of the rocks.

The girl took off her torn dress, shook her hair[57] and jumped into the pool. The water was clear and cool. She swam and stood under the waterfall and the water splashed onto her naked body.

Mary felt happy. One day she and Peter would reach Adelaide. She did not want to think about the bush boy. Today was beautiful. There was food to eat, water to drink. And Peter's cold was getting better. She started to sing.

While Mary was in the pool, Peter was putting more wood on the fire. It was burning brightly. And the bush boy had woken up.

The bush boy lay on his back, thinking. He was thinking about something very important. Did the strangers know how to make a burial platform? It must be high off the ground or the evil spirits would come out of the earth and take his body.

The bush boy slowly stood up. He would have to teach the strangers how to build the burial platform. He would have to hurry. He was getting weaker and weaker.

He wanted to talk to the little one, but Peter was away looking for wood. He heard the sound of the girl singing and splashing. He went to find her.

He climbed a rock and saw her in the pool below. She was naked and her hair was floating on the surface of the water. He saw for the first time that it was long and golden.

The bush boy had never seen such beautiful hair before. He lay down on the warm rock and stared in amazement.

Suddenly the girl looked up. She saw his staring eyes.

She moved backwards in terror. Her hands grabbed at a piece of rock. She pulled the rock free and held it tightly.

The bush boy came walking down to the billabong. But at the side of the pool he stopped in amazement. The girl was snarling[58] at him. She was snarling like an angry dog. Her eyes filled with terror.

The bush boy took another step forward. Then he saw the stone in the girl's hand and stopped again. The girl hated him. He could see that. He knew, in that moment, that his body would never be put upon a burial platform.

He felt suddenly weaker. Much weaker. He did not understand. He looked at the girl's frightened eyes and snarling mouth. And he was almost sick with shock. He no longer wanted to live.

He turned slowly. He walked back into the desert. Then he lay down in the shade of a mugga-wood tree.

To the bush people, the mugga-wood is the tree of sorrow[59]. Its branches hang to the ground and its flowers are always wet with a red juice[60]. This red juice runs from the flowers like drops of blood. The branches of the mugga-wood tree hung sadly over the bush boy. The juice from the large red flowers fell on the boy like drops of blood.

The bush boy had never seen such beautiful hair before.

14

Death

Peter was still putting wood on the fire when he saw his sister hurrying towards him. He knew something was wrong. She picked up a branch and began pushing sand onto the fire.

'Stop!' Peter was angry. 'You'll put it out.'

'We don't need the fire,' she said.

'Yes, we do,' said Peter. 'How are we going to cook our breakfast?'

'There's no breakfast,' she said. 'There's no food here. We can't stay. Let's go.'

Peter did not believe her. 'Why are you in such a hurry?' he said. 'The bush boy will find food.'

'Listen, Peter,' she said. 'Let's go on by ourselves. You and me. We'll be all right.'

Peter frowned. 'I don't want to leave the bush boy.'

'He doesn't want to come with us, Peter,' she said. 'I know he doesn't want to come. I asked him.'

'Are you sure?'

'I'm sure,' she replied.

But Peter still did not believe her. 'How did you ask him?' he asked. 'You can't talk to the bush boy!'

She went on pushing sand over the fire.

'I've told you,' she said. 'He doesn't want to come. I know.'

A week ago, Peter would have believed her. He would have done as she asked. But not now.

'I'm going to ask him myself.' He started walking off towards the rocks.

The girl started to run after him. Then she stopped. She sat down beside the fire.

After about ten minutes, Peter came running back.

'Hey, Mary!' His voice was frightened. 'The bush boy is ill. Very ill. He's lying under a tree. And he won't move.'

'Perhaps he's asleep.'

'He's *not* asleep. He's ill. Come and look.'

'No!' The girl shivered. 'No! I won't go near him.'

It was a long, sad day. Peter would not leave the bush boy, and Mary would not go near him. And they had no food.

Peter carried handfuls of water to the bush boy. At first, the bush boy would not drink. But after a while, he did drink a little.

The white children grew hungry. They looked in the pools for fish, but found none. Later they were lucky. They found some worwora balls. As the sun began to set, they cooked the worwora and ate them.

Peter took some to the bush boy, but he would not eat.

The bush boy was much weaker now. And he did not look at or listen to anything around him. But his cold was not worse and his fever had gone. He lay on the ground in silence. His dark eyes were almost closed. His body became colder and colder. He was waiting for Death.

Peter sat down beside the bush boy and held his hand. Peter had always liked the bush boy and he began to understand that his friend was dying. Peter held the boy's hand more tightly. After a while, the bush boy's lips began to move. Peter bent closer to listen.

'Arkooloola!' whispered the bush boy.

Peter ran down to the billabong, and brought back water in his hands. But the bush boy pushed Peter's hands away and shook his head. He slowly sat up on the ground.

'Arkooloola,' he whispered again and he pointed at Peter.

'Me?' The little boy was amazed. 'I don't want a drink.'

'Arkooloola,' the bush boy said again. 'Yeemara.' He pointed first at Peter, and then at the hills.

It was a long time before Peter understood. The bush boy pushed some sand with his hands. The sand looked like the hills.

Then he made a trail[61] from one side of the sand hills to the other. Suddenly Peter understood.

'Sure. Now I understand. There's food and water over the hills. Arkooloola and yeemara. That's fine. Now you lie down.'

The bush boy's eyes closed. He lay on his side and pulled up his knees. He lay still in the shade of the mugga-wood tree.

Peter stood up and walked across to his sister. She was sitting looking at the fire. As Peter came towards her, she looked up.

'How is he?' she asked.

'I think he'll soon be dead.'

'Oh, no! No! No! No!'

She held her hands over her face and started to move her body backwards and forwards.

Peter watched her and frowned. 'Mary,' he asked, 'do you think he will go to heaven[62]?'

'I don't believe you,' said Mary. 'He's only got a cold.'

'I don't think he'll go to heaven,' frowned Peter. 'He hasn't been baptised[63].'

The girl got up quickly. She started to walk up and down.

'Are you sure he's very ill, Peter?'

'Of course I'm sure,' the boy replied. 'Come and see.'

For a long time the girl was silent. Then she said slowly, 'Yes, I'll come.'

They walked across to the mugga-wood tree. The bush boy was lying in the shade. The girl sat down beside him and looked into his face. What Peter had said was true: the bush boy was dying.

Very gently, she lifted the bush boy's head onto her knees. Very softly, she began to move her fingers over and across his forehead.

The bush boy's eyes opened. For a moment he did not understand. Then he smiled.

That smile broke Mary's heart[64]. She knew she had been wrong and foolish. She should not have been afraid. The bush

Very gently, she lifted the bush boy's head onto her knees.

boy had never wanted to hurt her. She felt her fears disappear for ever. There was no difference between her and the bush boy. They did not come from different worlds. They were all part of one world – God's world.

The bush boy died as the sun came up. He died peacefully[65] in the hour when the desert is most silent.

Mary did not know he had died. She had fallen asleep. Her head lay on the sand and her cheek rested against the bush boy's cheek. And her long, golden hair had fallen across his face.

15

Mary and Peter Are All Alone

The desert sand was hard. The children had to dig a hole with pointed branches and sharp stones. Peter wanted the bush boy to go to heaven. So Mary said a prayer. Then Peter put some drops of water on the boy's forehead and baptised the bush boy.

They buried him close to the billabong.

By the time they had finished, it was midday. They were tired and hungry. They ate some food and sat looking at each other.

After a while Peter stood up.

'Come on, Mary,' he said. 'Kurura!'

'Where are we going to?' asked Mary.

'Over the hills, of course.'

'Are you sure that's the way, Peter?' asked the girl.

'Of course I'm sure. The bush boy told me. There's food and water over the hills.'

'All right,' she said. 'Let's go.' And they started to follow the stream.

They had learnt a lot from the bush boy. The ate berries, found food and made fire. They lived as he had lived. And they stayed alive.

During the day they did not speak about the bush boy. But now, as night came and they sat by the fire, they began to talk about him. Peter looked up at the sky. The stars were shining.

'Mary,' he whispered, 'is heaven up there? Is it above the stars?'

'That's right, Peter.'

'Do you think the bush boy is there?'

'Yes, Peter. I am sure he is.'

When the children woke next morning, they were hungry. They went down to the stream to look for fish. But they did not find any. So the two children jumped into the pool for a swim. Then they lay down beside the stream and the sun dried them.

But they could not stay by the pool for ever. Soon they were on their way again.

They followed the stream up the valley. The stream was smaller now and there were not so many trees and plants. The hills seemed a long, long way away.

Two hours before sunset they came to the beginning of the stream in a small valley. The ground was wet and there was no shade. Also, the pool of water was dirty. They could not drink it.

Then Mary remembered something the bush boy had taught them. She found a hollow reed[66] and put it deep under the dirty water. She sucked up clear, cool water.

They were not thirsty any more, but they were still hungry.

Peter began to move a reed about in the pool. Suddenly a little creature crawled out of the water.

'Hey, Mary! There's food in the pool.'

The girl came running over and looked at the little creature.

'He's very small, Peter,' she said.

'There might be more of them.'

Together they stared into the dirty water, but saw nothing.

'Mary!' said Peter. 'Do you remember how the bush boy killed all those fish by throwing stones? Shall we do that?'

'We can't do that here,' said Mary. 'The stones would stick in the mud.'

They stared sadly into the pool. Then the girl had an idea.

'I know. Let's move the mud about. Perhaps the creatures in the pool will climb out.'

They took some branches and moved the mud about. Soon the water became brown and muddy. Almost at once the small creatures came up to the surface. The children picked them up and killed them.

'That's enough, Peter. Let's not kill any more.'

They cooked the creatures on hot stones and they tasted delicious. There were still enough left for breakfast.

It was cooler on the high ground and they sat by the warm fire. The girl threw branches onto the fire and the flames flew up to the sky. Below in the valley, a dingo howled[67] at the moon.

16

Hunger and Thirst

Next morning, they killed some more creatures from the pool. They might need food for the journey in front of them. Then they started to walk to the hills.

The children walked for hours and hours. Every time they came to the top of a hill they stopped. They hoped to see the valley they were looking for. But they saw nothing but hills. Hills and more hills.

The land was very beautiful. They found some coloured stones and Mary wanted to take some with her.

'Come on,' Peter said. 'We can't eat stones.'

At midday they stopped for two hours and ate the rest of the water creatures. The creatures tasted salty, and the children had no water to drink. The sun was hot and the girl began to feel sleepy. But Peter was soon on his feet.

'Come on, Mary,' he said. 'Kurura. Perhaps the valley is over the next hill.'

But it wasn't. And there was no valley over the next hill. Or the next. Or the one after that.

That night they stopped beside a rock. They were hungry, thirsty, exhausted and afraid. There was no wood for a fire and no water to drink. The wind was cold.

Before they slept, the children talked in whispers.

'Peter!' The girl was worried. 'Do you think we should go back tomorrow? Back to the pool?'

'No!' said Peter. 'The bush boy said there's water over the hills. We'll go on.'

Next morning, the children woke up cold, hungry and thirsty.

'Come on, Mary,' whispered Peter. 'I don't like this place. Let's move on.'

Both children moved much more slowly than the day before. Every footstep was difficult.

Soon they came to some steep[68] rocks. At the top of the rocks, they saw little clouds. Where there were clouds, there was rain and water. Mary began to move more quickly and Peter did the same. But the rocks were very steep and they had to move carefully.

'Careful, Peter.' Mary pointed to the left. 'Let's go over there. It's not so steep.'

Slowly, painfully, they moved up higher.

There were more and more clouds. Mary began to get excited[69] and moved faster.

'We must be careful when we get to the top, Peter,' she said. 'The other side might be steep and dangerous.'

They reached the top together. A cool wind blew in their faces. And there below them was the Valley-of-waters-under-the-earth. The children stood hand in hand and looked.

The clouds almost covered the valley. But through the holes in the clouds they could see green trees and the shining water.

Peter danced with excitement.

'It's like the bush boy told us, Mary. Food and water. Yeemara and arkooloola.'

58

The girl nodded.

For a moment the clouds moved away. The children saw a large, beautiful river. Then the clouds came together again. But the children had seen the beautiful valley. Hand in hand, they went down into the Valley-of-waters-under-the-earth.

17

The Valley-of-Waters-Under-the-Earth

They went immediately to the pools of cool, delicious water and drank and drank.

Then they saw the birds.

The children had never seen so many birds. There were birds

everywhere – in the water, in the reeds, in the trees and in the sky. And the birds were singing.

At first the children were afraid of the dark forest. But later they became braver and walked into a strange, new world.

When they had been in the valley for three days they saw a koala bear[70].

'Look!' said Mary.

She pointed to one of the trees. A mother koala was sitting in the tree with her baby. Peter jumped forward. He grabbed the baby and put it into Mary's arms.

'Isn't it nice!' he grinned.

The mother koala moved too slowly to help her baby. But she did not run away. She started to moan[71].

Mary felt sorry for her. She tried to give the baby back to its mother. But the baby grabbed tightly at Mary's dress and pulled. The dress was torn to pieces, and fell to the ground at her feet. Mary gave the baby back to its mother. The mother stopped moaning immediately.

Mary was now standing completely naked. But she was not worried. She was more worried about the mother koala and her baby.

Later they stopped beside a lake[72]. The girl built a hut with reeds and the children stayed there for a few days.

Peter found some mud and they made some drawings on the rocks. Peter drew koalas and birds – and things he had seen on his journey. Mary drew girls' faces, their hair and their dresses. Her pictures were about things she had seen in America. Then she drew a house, a simple house. It had one door, one window, and a small garden with flowers.

That night, a bird sang in the forest and another bird answered out over the lake. The moon shone down and the valley was quiet.

Next morning, they got ready to leave. As they were starting to move away, they saw the smoke. Smoke from a fire on the other side of the lake.

18

The Bush People

T he children stared at the smoke in silence.
     Suddenly there were a number of puffs[73] of smoke. Mary turned to her brother. 'There's somebody over there!' she said.

The boy looked at the smoke and then at his sister. 'Shall we make smoke too?' he asked. 'Then they will know we are here.'

Mary nodded silently.

They brought a big branch with lots of leaves. Soon they were sending puffs of smoke into the air.

Mary stared across the lake. Suddenly she saw something move. Three people were swimming across the lake.

'They're coming, Peter.'

The boy stood by his sister. She was trembling, so he took her hand.

'Don't worry, Mary. I'll look after you.'

'Do you think they're white men, Peter? Or black, like the bush boy?'

I think they're like the bush boy, Mary,' answered Peter.

The girl nodded. She thought the same as Peter. Then she remembered that she was naked. But she was not worried. She was happy that they were black people and not white! She held Peter's hand and waited at the side of the lake.

The first swimmer was a man. A three-year-old baby was

sitting on his back. The baby was holding his father's hair with his fingers.

The second swimmer was a woman. She was carrying a dingo – a small wild dog.

The third swimmer was a girl about the same age as Mary. She was carrying a bag full of food.

The man came out of the water and put down his baby. He was a tall man with black hair. The baby had black skin and light hair. The three people were completely naked.

The man spoke to Peter. He was curious.

'Worum gala?' (Where do you come from?)

While Peter tried to speak to the man, the women turned to Mary.

The bush girl gave Mary some food. Mary took the present and gave the girl some fruit. The woman nodded and smiled. A few moments later, the baby started to cry. He wanted some of the food. Mary picked him up and the baby stopped crying. He began to play with her long, golden hair. Soon all three were smiling together.

Peter stopped talking to the bush man. The little boy was looking at the dingo. He loved dogs. Suddenly he ran after the dog and started playing with it in the water.

The bush man laughed. He looked round and saw the children's drawings.

He looked at Peter's drawings of koalas and birds. Then he saw Mary's drawings. He stared at them in amazement.

Where had these strangers come from? At last he saw the drawing of the house.

'Awhee! Awhee!'

The woman came across quickly and they stared at the drawing of the house. The two bush people looked at Mary and then at the house.

'Awhee! Awhee!'

The woman was excited. She pointed to the drawing of the

'Worum gala?' (Where do you come from?)

house and pointed to the hills on the other side of the valley. Suddenly Mary understood. Over the hills, there was a house – a white man's house.

'Where? Where?'

The bush man took the white girl by the hand and walked down to the side of the lake.

Peter saw them together and stopped playing with the dog. He came and stood at his sister's side.

He watched the bush man point to a valley in the hills. The children understood. They must climb to the top of the valley and then rest for the night. The bush man made a drawing in the sand. He drew more hills, pools of water and places with food. At last, the man drew a house, a white man's house: a door, a window, a garden with flowers.

The white children looked at each other.

'Oh, Peter!'

She suddenly started to cry.

Peter looked at the dog and the trees and the lake. He knew he would remember them for the rest of his life. Then he walked slowly to the fire and picked up the rest of their food. He stood for a moment and looked up the valley. Then he went across to the bush man and held out his hand.

'Goodbye!' he said.

The bush man grinned and he too held out his hand.

Peter turned to the girl.

'Come on, Mary,' he said. 'Kurura.'

He started to walk towards the valley.

Points for Understanding

1

1 Mary and Peter were the only passengers on the plane.
  (a) How old was Mary? And Peter?
  (b) Where had they come from?
  (c) Where were they going to?
  (d) Who were they going to visit there?
2 When the plane hit the ground, the flames spread everywhere.
  (a) What did Mary and Peter do?
  (b) What happened to the pilot and co-pilot?

2

1 How did the children get water?
2 How much food did the children have?
3 Where were the children lost?

3

1 What is 'the bush'?
2 Mary suddenly remembered that she had no clothes on. Why did Mary get dressed so quickly?
3 Mary gave Peter the piece of barley sugar.
  (a) How much did she eat herself?
  (b) How much food did the children have left now?

4

1 Mary was surprised that Peter had remembered all this.
  (a) What had Peter remembered?
  (b) What did Mary decide to do?
  (c) What did the children not know?
2 Peter shouted, 'It's the sea! We haven't got far to go.' Why was Mary upset?
3 What food did the children find?

4 'I think someone is watching us,' said Peter.
   (a) Who was watching them?
   (b) Why did Mary scream with fright?

5

1 What seemed shocking and wrong to Mary about the bush boy?
2 They were people from different worlds.
   (a) Who were the bush boy's people?
   (b) What was the great difference between these people and people
       in America?
3 Peter decided to do the same as his sister.
   (a) What was Mary doing?
   (b) What did Peter do which made the bush boy start laughing?
4 Why was Mary afraid of the bush boy touching her?
5 'Mary,' said Peter in a frightened voice. 'He's gone!'
   (a) Why was Mary pleased and sorry at the same time?
   (b) Who made a decision?
   (c) What was the decision?

6

1 How did Peter learn his first words of the bush boy's langauge?
2 At first, Mary did not want to leave the forest.
   (a) What could Mary see in front of them?
   (b) Why did the bush boy speak quietly to the children?
   (c) What did Mary see near the rocks which made her change her
       mind?
3 How did Mary learn the right way to drink the water from the pool?
4 Why did the bush boy clear away the leaves and twigs from the place
   where he was going to light a fire?
5 How did the bush boy make a fire?

7

1 'I don't need clothes, Mary,' Peter said to his sister.
   (a) What did Mary say in reply?
   (b) What did Peter agree to do?

2 Mary was happy. The bush boy was no longer naked.
   (a) What did Mary give to the bush boy?
   (b) Why did Peter start laughing and dancing up and down?
   (c) What did the bush boy do?
   (d) What happened to Mary's gift to the bush boy?
3 Mary's eyes were filled with terror.
   (a) What had the bush boy noticed about Mary?
   (b) Why did Mary's eyes fill with terror?
   (c) What did the bush boy think Mary had seen?
   (d) What did the boy decide was going to happen to him?

8

1 What did the Aborigine people believe about death and what
   happened after death?
2 Mary and Peter did not know that the bush boy had been on his
   Walkabout.
   (a) What is a 'Walkabout'?
   (b) Why did the Aborigine people make their young boys go on a
       Walkabout?
   (c) What did the bush boy now believe about his Walkabout?
   (d) What did the bush boy do?
3 Why did the bush boy let Peter look into his eyes? What did Peter do
   when the bush boy stared at him?
4 The bush boy began to think about the strangers.
   (a) What would happen to the children if the bush boy left them?
   (b) What did the bush boy decide to do?

9

1 Mary would not go near the bush boy. What did she do whenever he
   looked at her?
2 The bush boy took the bustard to the girl.
   (a) Why did the bush boy think Mary should carry the dead bird?
   (b) How did Mary feel while she was carrying the bird?
3 The bush boy did not sleep all night. What was he thinking about?
4 The bush people have a terrible weakness. What was this weakness?
5 The bush boy had seen the same terror twice before.
   (a) When had he seen it in the eyes of a woman?
   (b) When had he seen it in the eyes of an old man?

1 The dust made Peter sneeze.
    (a) What was wrong with Peter?
    (b) What did the bush boy think was wrong with Peter?
    (c) What did the bush boy do as he was going to sleep?
2 The bush boy found a pool of fish.
    (a) How did Peter try to catch the fish?
    (b) What did the fish do when Peter tried to catch them?
    (c) How did the bush boy catch the fish?
    (d) How did the children carry the fish back to the fire?
3 Mary told her brother to wash his trousers and put them on.
    (a) What did Peter reply?
    (b) What did the bush boy do with the trousers?

11

1 The bush boy showed the children an ordinary, brown bird. What two very unusual things did the children learn about the 'ordinary, brown bird'?
2 In the evening the bush boy sang and danced.
    (a) What was the bush boy pretending to be?
    (b) What happened in the middle of the dance?
    (c) What did the bush boy remember about the old man who had sneezed?
3 That night the bush boy did not sleep. What was wrong with him?

12

1 The midday rest was longer than usual.
    (a) Why was the rest longer than usual?
    (b) What did the white children have to do?
2 The bush boy was afraid that the children did not know how to build a burial platform.
    (a) What was a 'burial platform'?
    (b) Why did the platform have to be built high off the ground?
3 Peter asked Mary to give the bush boy her dress.
    (a) Why did Peter ask Mary to do this?
    (b) What was Mary's reply?
    (c) Why did Mary wish that her brother was a few years older?

13

1 The bush boy wanted to teach the children how to build a burial platform.
 (a) Why was he in a hurry to teach them?
 (b) Why did he not speak to Peter about the platform?
 (c) Why did the bush boy stare at Mary in amazement?
 (d) What did Mary do when she saw the bush boy staring at her?
2 Why was the bush boy certain that his body would never be put on a burial platform?
3 What kind of tree was the mugga-wood tree?

14

1 'Let's go on by ourselves,' Mary said to Peter.
 (a) Did Peter agree with her?
 (b) What did Mary tell Peter the bush boy wanted to do?
 (c) Why did Peter not believe his sister?
2 'Arkooloola,' the bush boy said again. 'Yeemara.'
 (a) Where did the bush boy point as he was saying these words?
 (b) What did the bush boy do with some sand?
 (c) What did Peter understand from the bush boy's sign language?
3 Mary sat down beside the bush boy and looked into his face.
 (a) What did Mary understand?
 (b) What did Mary do?
 (c) How did Mary feel when the bush boy smiled at her?
4 Mary understood that the white children and the bush boy did not come from different worlds. What world were they all part of?

15

1 Why did Peter baptise the bush boy?
2 'Do you think the bush boy is there?' Peter asked his sister.
 (a) Where did Peter mean by 'there'?
 (b) What was Mary's reply?
3 Mary and Peter had learnt a lot from the bush boy. After the bush boy died, they were able to keep alive in the desert. Give two examples of how they remembered something the bush boy had taught them.

16

1 Mary was worried and asked Peter, 'Do you think we should go back?'
    (a) Why was Mary worried?
    (b) What was Peter's reply?
2 Why did the children move more quickly when they saw the clouds?
3 'It's like the bush boy told us, Mary,' said Peter. What were the children looking at when Peter said this?

17

1 Mary was now standing completely naked.
    (a) What did the baby koala bear do to Mary's dress?
    (b) Why was Mary not worried?
2 The children made drawings on the rocks.
    (a) What kind of things did Peter draw?
    (b) What kind of things did Mary draw?
3 What did the children see as they were starting to move away?

18

1 The bush man and woman stared at Mary's drawings.
    (a) What drawing made them very excited?
    (b) What did the bush woman do?
    (c) What did Mary understand?
2 The bush man made a drawing in the sand.
    (a) What did the bush man draw?
    (b) Why did Mary start to cry?

Glossary

1 **gasp** (page 5)
to make a noise by breathing inwards quickly.

2 **spread** (page 5)
when a fire spreads the flames move from one place to another.

3 **sinking** – *kept sinking* (page 5)
each time he walked forward, Peter's feet went down into the soft sand. To keep doing something is to do something again and again.

4 **explode** (page 5)
when a bomb goes off it explodes. The fuel in the aeroplane exploded like a bomb.

5 **trembling** – *to tremble* (page 7)
when you are ill or afraid your body shakes and trembles.

6 **whisper** (page 7)
to speak quietly.

7 **sugar** – *stick of barley sugar* (page 7)
a hard sweet made from sugar.

8 **fox** – *flying fox* (page 8)
an animal with wings which eats fruit. See the illustration on page 4.

9 **firefly** (page 8)
an insect whose body shines in the dark like a light. See the illustration on page 4.

10 **wombat** (page 8)
a large Australian animal, covered in fur. See the illustration on page 4.

11 **den** (page 8)
a place where an animal lives.

12 **shrub** (page 8)
a small bush.

13 **naked** (page 9)
without clothes.

14 **yelled** – *to yell* (page 9)
to shout loudly.

15 **ant** (page 11)
small insect with six legs that lives in the ground.

16 **berry** (page 12)
a small fruit that grows on trees or bushes.

17 **mud** (page 13)
soft wet earth.

18 **poisonous** (page 14)
if something is poisonous and you eat it you will become ill and could die.
19 **nervous** (page 15)
to feel worried and afraid.
20 **fright** – *almost screamed with fright* (page 15)
Mary wanted to shout out loudly in fear but did not do so.
21 **grab** – *to grab* (page 15)
to catch something quickly with your hand and hold onto it.
22 **weapon** (page 15)
something used in a fight. For example, a spear or a gun.
23 **wallaby** (page 17)
a small Australian animal that has a long tail and runs on two legs.
See the illustration on page 4.
24 **shocking** (page 17)
something which makes you feel very upset and worried.
25 **stare** (page 17)
to look at someone for a long time.
26 **crop** (page 17)
a plant that is grown for food.
27 **creature** (page 17)
creatures are people or animals. The bush boy had never seen white children before, and was not sure if they were people or animals.
28 **amazement** – *to watch in amazement* (page 18)
to look at something because you find it very strange.
29 **frowned** – *to frown* (page 18)
to move your face to show you are angry or do not understand something.
30 **grinned** – *to grin* (page 18)
to give a big friendly smile.
31 **pretend** – *to pretend to drink* (page 21)
Peter put his hands to his mouth showing that he wanted to drink.
But he had no water in his hands.
32 **got it** – *You've got it* (page 22)
you have understood.
33 **chew** – *pretended to chew* (page 22)
chewing is the movement your mouth makes when you are eating.
Peter moved his mouth to show the bush boy that he wanted to eat.
34 **forest** (page 22)
a large number of trees growing together.

35 *exhausted* (page 23)
very, very tired.
36 *spirits – evil spirits* (page 23)
bad spirits (see Gloss. no. 44).
37 *fern* (page 23)
a tall green plant that grows near wet ground.
38 *twig* (page 25)
a small branch from a tree or a bush.
39 *jealous – to feel jealous* (page 25)
to be upset because someone is more interested in another person than in you.
40 *saved – saved their lives* (page 27)
if the bush boy had not helped them the children would have died in the desert.
41 *present –* (page 28)
something you give to someone to show you like them.
42 *spear* (page 29)
a long pointed stick used as a *weapon* (see Gloss. no. 22).
43 *terror* (page 31)
very great fear. The bush boy saw this great fear in the girl's eyes.
44 *Death – Spirit of Death* (page 31)
Australian aborigines believed that there were spirits all around them. No one could see these spirits, but they were there. They were in the earth, in the sky, in the rivers and in the trees. Some of these spirits were bad. One of the bad spirits was the Spirit of Death. When a person was sick, the Spirit of Death came to take life away from that person and he died.
45 *language – sign language* (page 36)
the bush boy and Peter did not speak the same language. To make Peter understand what he was saying, the bush boy made signs with his hands.
46 *plateau* (page 38)
a high, flat piece of land.
47 *sniffed – to sniff* (page 39)
to breathe loudly through your nose.
48 *remarkable* (page 42)
strange and wonderful.
49 *shivering – to shiver* (page 44)
the movement your body makes when you are cold or afraid.

50 **well** – *not well* (page 45)
the boy feels ill.

51 **platform** – *burial platform* (page 45)
the Australian Aborigines believed that there were bad spirits who took away the bodies of dead people. To stop these evil spirits taking their bodies, the Aborigines used branches of trees to build burial platforms high above the ground. They put the dead body on the burial platform (see Gloss. no. 44).

52 **plain** (page 46)
flat land.

53 **selfish** (page 46)
to think only of yourself and not to worry about other people.

54 **cowardly** (page 46)
easily made afraid.

55 **billabong** (page 47)
an Australian word for a pool of water.

56 **waterfall** (page 47)
water falling from a high place.

57 **hair** – *shook her hair* (page 47)
Mary moves her head so that her hair is away from her face.

58 **snarl** (page 48)
to open your mouth and make a noise like an angry dog.

59 **sorrow** (page 48)
great sadness.

60 **juice** (page 48)
the liquid inside a fruit.

61 **trail** (page 52)
the bush boy marks the ground, to show a path in his drawing.

62 **heaven** (page 52)
the place where religious people believe they go when they die.

63 **baptised** (page 52)
to baptise someone, a priest puts some water on a person's forehead and gives them a name. Christians believe you have to be baptised before you go to heaven (see above).

64 **heart** – *broke Mary's heart* (page 52)
Mary was so sad that she felt a pain in her heart.

65 **peacefully** (page 54)
quietly and happily.

66 **reed** – *hollow reed* (page 56)

a tall plant that grows by the water and has a hole down the middle of its stem.

67 **howled** – *to howl* (page 57)

dogs and some other animals make a long loud noise when they howl.

68 **steep** (page 58)

the rocks have high sides.

69 **excited** – *to get excited* (page 58)

you are excited when you feel something interesting and important is going to happen.

70 **bear** – *koala bear* (page 60)

a small bear that lives in the trees in Australia.

71 **moan** (page 60)

to make a sad noise.

72 **lake** (page 60)

a very large pool of water.

73 **puffs** (page 61)

little clouds of smoke coming up from a fire.

INTERMEDIATE LEVEL

Shane *by Jack Schaefer*
Old Mali and the Boy *by D. R. Sherman*
Bristol Murder *by Philip Prowse*
Tales of Goha *by Leslie Caplan*
The Smuggler *by Piers Plowright*
The Pearl *by John Steinbeck*
Things Fall Apart *by Chinua Achebe*
The Woman Who Disappeared *by Philip Prowse*
The Moon is Down *by John Steinbeck*
A Town Like Alice *by Nevil Shute*
The Queen of Death *by John Milne*
Walkabout *by James Vance Marshall*
Meet Me in Istanbul *by Richard Chisholm*
The Great Gatsby *by F. Scott Fitzgerald*
The Space Invaders *by Geoffrey Matthews*
My Cousin Rachel *by Daphne du Maurier*
I'm the King of the Castle *by Susan Hill*
Dracula *by Bram Stoker*
The Sign of Four *by Sir Arthur Conan Doyle*
The Speckled Band and Other Stories *by Sir Arthur Conan Doyle*
The Eye of the Tiger *by Wilbur Smith*
The Queen of Spades and Other Stories *by Aleksandr Pushkin*
The Diamond Hunters *by Wilbur Smith*
When Rain Clouds Gather *by Bessie Head*
Banker *by Dick Francis*
No Longer at Ease *by Chinua Achebe*
The Franchise Affair *by Josephine Tey*
The Case of the Lonely Lady *by John Milne*

For further information on the full selection of
Readers at all five levels in the series, please refer
to the Heinemann Guided Readers catalogue.

Heinemann International
A division of Heinemann Publishers (Oxford) Ltd
Halley Court, Jordan Hill, Oxford OX2 8EJ

OXFORD LONDON EDINBURGH
MADRID ATHENS BOLOGNA PARIS
MELBOURNE SYDNEY AUCKLAND SINGAPORE TOKYO
IBADAN NAIROBI HARARE GABORONE
PORTSMOUTH (NH)

ISBN 0 435 27247 0

First published as *The Children* by Michael Joseph 1959
© Michael Joseph 1959
This retold version for Heinemann Guided Readers
© Jim Alderson 1979, 1992
First published 1979
Reprinted six times
This edition published 1992

Illustrated by Trevor Parkin
Typography by Adrian Hodgkins
Cover by Sarah Ball and Threefold Design
Typeset in 11/12.5 pt Goudy
by Joshua Associates Ltd, Oxford
Printed and bound in Malta

93 94 95 96 97 10 9 8 7 6 5 4 3 2